PAPERBACK

M000106675

Table of Contents

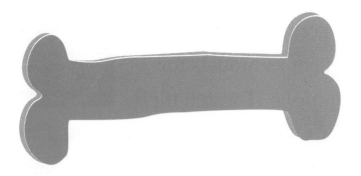

Meet
Cynthia Rylant

"I have two dogs. Martha Jane is a big marshmallow dog who loves to be held. Leia, named after Princess Leia in *Star Wars*, is little and always running in circles. We call her a 'little sausage.' I also have two cats, Blueberry and Edward Velvetpaws."

Meet
Suçie Stevenson

Suçie Stevenson says, "I have a great many dog pals and use them as models for my illustrations. I watch their expressions and movements when they roughhouse." Two of her best models are her own Labrador retrievers.

Henry and Mudge
AND THE
Happy Cat

The Eighth Book of Their Adventures

Story by Cynthia Rylant
Pictures by Suçie Stevenson

HOUGHTON MIFFLIN COMPANY
BOSTON
ATLANTA   DALLAS   GENEVA, ILLINOIS   PALO ALTO   PRINCETON

To the Peacocks: Nancy,
Larry, Aaron, and Natalie—CR

For Chuck, Kathy, and Jack—SS

Acknowledgments

For each of the selections listed below, grateful acknowledgment is made for permission to excerpt and/or reprint original or copyrighted materials, as follows:

Selections

"Ask Cynthia Rylant," from Preview Issue of *Storyworks* magazine, Spring 1993. Copyright © 1993 by Scholastic, Inc. Reprinted by permission.

"Blossom the School Cat," by Marsha Arnold, from January/February 1993 *U*S* Kids, A Weekly Reader Magazine.* Copyright © 1992 by Children's Better Health Institute, Benjamin Franklin Literary & Medical Society, Inc., Indianapolis, Indiana. Reprinted by permission.

Henry and Mudge and the Happy Cat, by Cynthia Rylant. Text copyright © 1990 by Cynthia Rylant. Illustrations copyright © 1990 by Suçie Stevenson. Reprinted by permission of Macmillan Books for Young Readers, Simon & Schuster Children's Publishing Division.

Excerpt adapted from *Who Says a Dog Goes Bow-Wow?* by Hank De Zutter. Text copyright © 1993 by Hank De Zutter. Illustrations copyright © 1993 by Suse MacDonald. Reprinted by permission of Bantam Doubleday Dell Books for Young Readers.

Photography

ii Richard C. Owens Publishers, Inc. (t); courtesy of Suçie Stevenson (b). **49** Drew Endicott (cover). **49–52** Courtesy of Apple Blossom School. **49, 50–51, 52** Tony Scarpetta.

2001 Impression
Houghton Mifflin Edition, 1996
Copyright © 1996 by Houghton Mifflin Company. All rights reserved.

Printed in the U.S.A.

ISBN: 0-395-73220-4

17 18 19 20-B-08 07 06

Contents

What Is It?

One night Henry
and Henry's father
and Henry's big dog Mudge
were watching TV.

Suddenly Mudge ran
to the door
and barked.

Henry's father opened
the door. Sitting
on the steps was
the shabbiest cat
Henry had ever seen.

It had a saggy belly,
skinny legs,
and fur that looked like
mashed prunes.
Henry and Henry's father
and Henry's big dog Mudge
stood in the door
and looked at the shabby cat.
"Hey kitty," said Henry.
"Are you sure it's a kitty?"
said Henry's father.

"It might be a stray,"
Henry said, petting it.
"It has to be," said Henry's father.
"That is the shabbiest cat
I have ever seen."

He carried the cat
into the house while
Henry and Mudge followed.
Mudge's tail was wagging hard.

"This cat looks like
mashed prunes," said Henry.
"But it's nice."
"Nice for a disaster,"
said Henry's father.

The three of them watched
as the cat drank three
bowls of milk in a row.

"Can it stay?" Henry asked.
"Only until we find a home
for it," said his father.
He looked hard at the cat.

"Do you think it *knows*
it's that shabby?" Henry's father asked.

Mudge was licking some milk

from the visitor's chin.

"Mudge doesn't know,"

Henry said.

"Mudge likes it."

"Yes," said Henry's father,

"but Mudge also likes turkey gizzards."

A Good Mother

In one week the shabby cat
turned into a happy cat.
It loved three things
about Henry's house.
It loved the towel closet.
It loved the bathtub.

And it loved Mudge.

In one week
the shabby cat had become
Mudge's mother.

It washed Mudge all the time.
It washed Mudge's ears.
It washed Mudge's eyes.
It even washed Mudge's dirty feet.
"*Yuck,*" said Henry.

The cat also made Mudge
use good manners.
Mudge had to wait his turn
at the water dish.

Mudge had to share
his dog toys.

Mudge even had to share his crackers.
But Mudge didn't mind,
because Mudge loved the cat, too.

Henry's mother and Henry's father
wondered what they would do
with the cat.
They liked it.
But taking care of Mudge
was like taking care
of five dogs.
They didn't want
any more pets.

Henry's mother decided to make
posters to find a home
for the cat.
Henry helped her.

"Don't put the cat's picture
on them," said Henry's father,
"or we'll have that cat forever."

Henry and Mudge walked
around town with the posters.
They put one in
the grocery store
and one in the drugstore
and one in the record store.

24

They put a lot of them
on trees.
And Mudge ate one
by mistake.
The posters didn't say
anything about mashed prunes.

When Henry and Mudge
came home,
Henry's father and Henry's mother
were sitting on the couch
with the cat.

Henry's mother said,
"Cats are nice."
Henry's father said,
"Even shabby ones."

Mudge climbed onto the couch

to be with his new mother.

Henry climbed on next.

The happy cat purred and purred.

A Surprise

A lot of people saw the posters
and came to look
at the cat.

Some of them
were very rude.
They made fun of the cat.
Mudge watched them,
and his fur stood up.

A lot of people came to see
the cat because
they had lost their own.

But they always said,
"Ours is white."

Or,

"Ours is gray."

No one ever said,
"Ours looks like mashed prunes."
No one seemed to want
the cat.

Then one day
there was a surprise.
A police car parked
in front of Henry's house,
and a policeman rang
Henry's bell.

Henry and Henry's father
and Henry's big dog Mudge
went to the door.
"Can I help you?"
Henry's father asked the policeman.
(Henry's father was wondering if
Mudge had eaten somebody's purse.)

But the policeman had seen one
of the posters.
He was looking for his cat.

He said it was different
from other cats.
He said it was "unique."
He said it looked something
like mashed prunes.

Henry ran to get
the cat.
When he came back with it,
the policeman cried, "Dave!"
Henry and Henry's father
looked at each other.
"*Dave?*" said Henry's father.

Dave jumped out of Henry's arms
and into the policeman's arms.
The policeman kissed Dave
on the nose.
"I'm so happy to have him
back," the policeman said.

Henry looked at Mudge,
who was looking at Dave.
"Your cat likes our dog,"
Henry told the policeman.

The policeman looked at Mudge.
"I can see that," he said.
"Your dog has very clean ears."
Suddenly Henry got a
lump in his throat.
He didn't want Mudge
to lose his mother.
Even if Mudge's mother
was named Dave.

The policeman said good-bye,
and he took
his happy cat home.
When Dave the cat was gone,
Henry and Mudge felt very sad.

The towel closet was shut.

The bathtub was empty.

The dog toys were still.

43

Henry had to cry a little
and take a nap.
Mudge had to eat a lot of crackers
and take a nap.

Henry's father and Henry's mother
had to give them both extra hugs.

The next day
a big box was on their porch.
The note on it said:

TO MUDGE FROM DAVE.

Inside the box

were thirty giant dog bones!

And under those

was a gold police badge!

Mudge kept the dog bones
for himself.
But he shared the police badge
with Henry.
Dave the cat had taught him
very good manners.

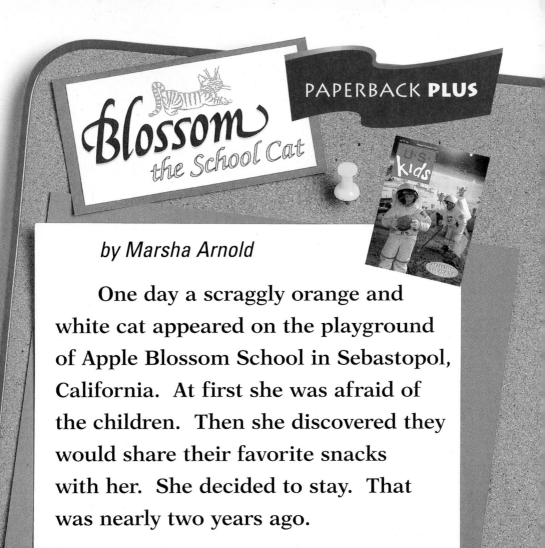

Blossom
the School Cat

by Marsha Arnold

One day a scraggly orange and white cat appeared on the playground of Apple Blossom School in Sebastopol, California. At first she was afraid of the children. Then she discovered they would share their favorite snacks with her. She decided to stay. That was nearly two years ago.

The children named her Blossom after their school.

Blossom is now the school mascot. Her picture decorates the school T-shirt. You can see it on the school's daily bulletin, along with the words: "Apple Blossom School, Home of Blossom."

Blossom has her own morning routine. At 6:00 A.M., she visits the cafeteria. She waits politely outside the kitchen door for tasty tidbits from the cook.

Later in the morning, Blossom visits the principal's office. Sometimes the principal is in a conference. Blossom curls up on top of the coats and sweaters in the Lost and Found Box and waits.

In the afternoon, Blossom visits the classrooms. She sees how the children's lessons are going.

Sometimes *Blossom* is the lesson! One class created a counting book about Blossom and what she likes to eat.

Another class voted Blossom "Very

Important Cat of the Week." Each student wrote a story about her. Then they had their pictures taken with their *purr-fect* school cat.

Once in a while, Blossom gets so comfortable in a classroom that she falls asleep. The teacher may forget and lock Blossom inside the school at the end of the day. But the custodian always finds her and lets her outside for the evening.

"Having a school cat shows we care not only about kids, but about animals, too," says the principal. "A school that has a school cat is a very special school."

Blossom thinks so, too. After all, most cats have only one owner to take care of them.

Blossom has 563!

Who Says a Dog Goes Bow-Wow?

by Hank De Zutter
illustrated by Suse MacDonald

Who says a dog goes "bow-wow"?
Not the dog.
And who says a pig goes "oink-oink"?
Not the hog.

In Britain, for instance, or the U.S. of A.,
A dog barks "bow-wow," or so people say.

But the same dog in Germany, Greece, or Japan
Barks with a "woo-woo," "gav-gav," or "wan-wan."

How does a dog bark?

How-how	Finnish, Turkish, Russian, Polish
Huf-huf	Hebrew, Farsi
Vow-vow	Danish
Wan-wan	Japanese
Wah-wah	French
Woof-woof	Dutch

Bow-bow	Italian
Hong-hong	Thai
Mong-mong	Korean
Wang-wang	Chinese
Woo-woo	Swahili
Wow-wow	Spanish
Bow-wow	English

54